Peeper
and
Zeep

I Like to Read® books, created by award-winning
picture book artists as well as talented newcomers,
instill confidence and the joy of reading in new readers.

We want to hear every new reader say, "I like to read!"

_____

Visit our website for flash cards, activities, and more about the series:
www.holidayhouse.com/ILiketoRead
#ILTR

This book has been tested by an educational expert
and determined to be a guided reading level E.

Peeper

and
Zeep

Adam Gudeon

I Like to Read®

HOLIDAY HOUSE • NEW YORK

To my parents—
Loretta and Marvin,
Arthur and Susan

I LIKE TO READ is a registered trademark of Holiday House, Inc.

Copyright © 2017 by Adam Gudeon
All Rights Reserved
HOLIDAY HOUSE is registered in the U.S. Patent and Trademark Office.
Printed and Bound in July 2018 at Tien Wah Press, Johor Bahru, Johor, Malaysia.
The artwork was created with ink and digital coloring.
www.holidayhouse.com
First Edition
3 5 7 9 10 8 6 4 2

Library of Congress Cataloging-in-Publication Data
Names: Gudeon, Adam, author.
Title: Peeper and Zeep / Adam Gudeon.
Description: First edition. | New York : Holiday House, [2017] | Series: I
like to read | Summary: "Peeper, a chick who has injured his wing, and
Zeep, an alien who has crashed his spaceship, hope Frog, an inventor can
help them return to their homes"— Provided by publisher.
Identifiers: LCCN 2016004120 | ISBN 9780823436743 (hardcover)
Subjects: | CYAC: Chickens—Fiction. | Animals—Infancy—Fiction. |
Extraterrestrial beings—Fiction. | Frogs—Fiction. | Helpfulness—Fiction.
Classification: LCC PZ7.G93495 Pe 2017 | DDC [E]—dc23 LC record available at
https://lccn.loc.gov/2016004120

ISBN 978-0-8234-3779-5 (paperback)

This is Peeper.

This is Zeep.

Peeper fell.

He broke his wing.

Zeep fell. He broke his spaceship.

Peeper is lost.

Zeep is lost.

Peeper and Zeep meet.

How will Peeper get home?
How will Zeep get home?

Can Frog help?

Peeper and Zeep go up.

Peeper and Zeep go down.

Frog will try again.

Peeper and Zeep go up.

They go and go.

They stop.

Frog must try again.

Peeper, Zeep
and Frog
rest first.

Now they all try.

Now they all work.

Peeper and Zeep have a nice new home.
They wait.

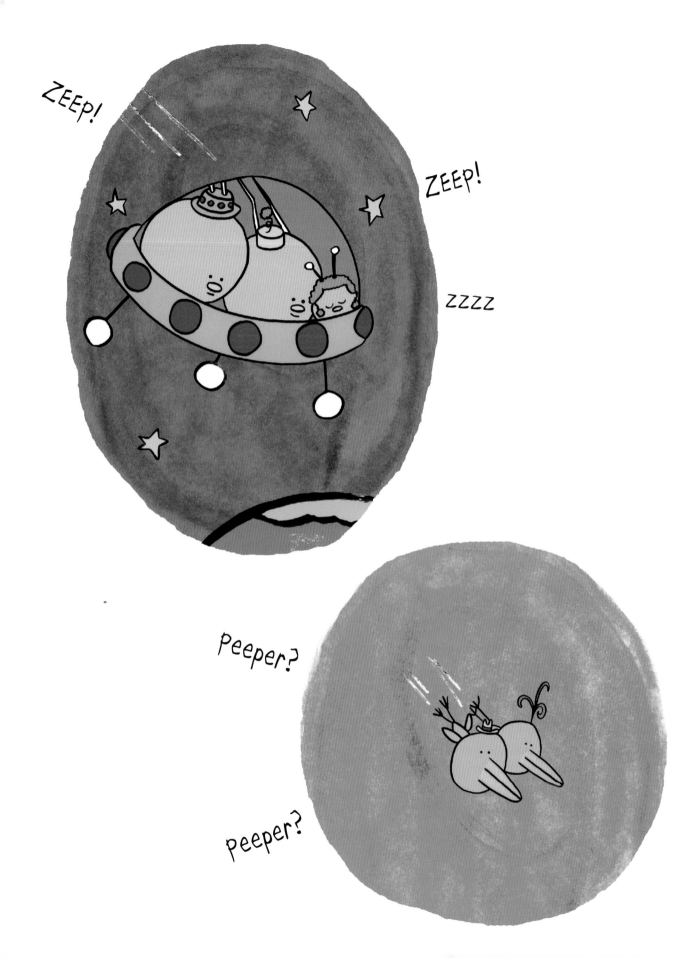

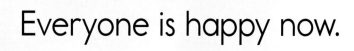

Everyone is happy now.

You will like these too!

Come Back, Ben by Ann Hassett and John Hassett
A *Kirkus Reviews* Best Book

Dinosaurs Don't, Dinosaurs Do by Steve Björkman
A Notable Social Studies Trade Book for Young People
An IRA/CBC Children's Choice

Fish Had a Wish by Michael Garland
A *Kirkus Reviews* Best Book
A Top 25 Children's Books list book

The Fly Flew In by David Catrow
An IRA/CBC Children's Choice
Maryland Blue Crab Young Reader Award Winner

Look! by Ted Lewin
The Correll Book Award for Excellence
in Early Childhood Informational Text

Me Too! by Valeri Gorbachev
A Bank Street Best Book of the Year

Mice on Ice by Rebecca Emberley and Ed Emberley
A Bank Street Best Children's Book of the Year
An IRA/CBC Children's Choice

Pig Has a Plan by Ethan Long
An IRA/CBC Children's Choice

See Me Dig by Paul Meisel
A *Kirkus Reviews* Best Book

See Me Run by Paul Meisel
A Theodor Seuss Geisel Award Honor Book
An ALA Notable Children's Book

You Can Do It by Betsy Lewin
A Bank Street Best Children's Book of the Year,
Outstanding Merit

See more I Like to Read® books.
Go to www.holidayhouse.com/I-Like-to-Read